Books should be returned or renewed by the last date above. Renew by phone **03000 41 31 31** or online *www.kent.gov.uk/libs*

PENELOPE STRUDEL
AND THE
BIRTHDAY
TREASURE
HUNT

BY BRENDAN KEARNEY

Frances Lincoln
Children's Books

EST. 1902

Custard Manor
Trifle Hill
Puddington

Dearest Penelope,

Happy birthday and welcome to Custard Manor! We've all been awaiting your arrival with great excitement. Crumble the Dog and Lawrence the Cat haven't stopped talking about your trip since they found out you were coming!

I've got a special birthday surprise waiting for you somewhere but those pesky puffins that love fluttering around my lovely manor have been causing havoc lately. To make sure they don't get their feathery mitts on your surprise, I've hidden it somewhere safe for you. Follow the clues I've laid out and you'll find it in no time!

In each room there is a letter you need to find that contains a clue to help you on your birthday quest. You'll have to solve a puzzle to bring you to the next room before those perpetually pooing puffins beat you to it... Your birthday surprise depends on it!

And remember to keep an eye out for those mischievous puffins – there are 11 in every room! Find them before they find your surprise!

Good luck and let the Birthday Treasure Hunt begin!

lots of love,

Uncle
Derek Custard

xx

TOP SECRET
FAO: Penelope
Strudel

Greetings! I am the Puffin King, ruler of all puffins! I'm hiding somewhere in Custard Manor – I bet you can't find me!

CUSTARD MANOR
Floor plan

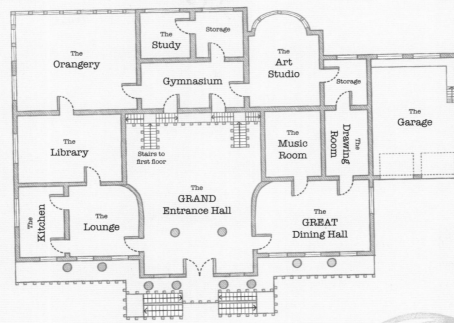

Ground Floor

The Orangery

The Study — Storage

Gymnasium

The Art Studio

Storage

The Garage

The Library

The Music Room

The Drawing Room

Stairs to first floor

The GRAND Entrance Hall

The Kitchen

The Lounge

The GREAT Dining Hall

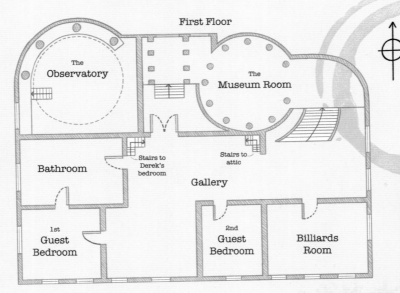

First Floor

The Observatory

The Museum Room

Bathroom

Stairs to Derek's bedroom

Stairs to attic

Gallery

1st Guest Bedroom

2nd Guest Bedroom

Billiards Room

CLUE ONE:

Here is the first clue to get you started on your birthday surprise quest. Unscramble the letters to find the name of the first room you need to visit. Good luck!

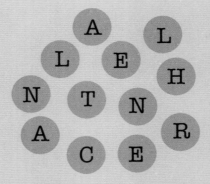

A L E L H
N T N H
A C E R

REMEMBER:

Find everything on the checklist

Find and stop those pesky puffins

Find the hidden letter

Solve the clues to guide you to the next room

And don't forget to have a piece of paper ready to write down the answers to the clues!

The Entrance Hall

By Jove you've solved the first clue already! Great stuff old sport. I started you off with an easy one but it's clear that these clues are no match for your brilliant brain! This is the entrance hall to my grand manor but as you can see those problematic puffins have been busy making a terrible mess. Tina the Seal has the letter containing your next clue – can you find her amongst the utter chaos? Remember to tick off everything on the checklist before moving on with your quest.

Derek

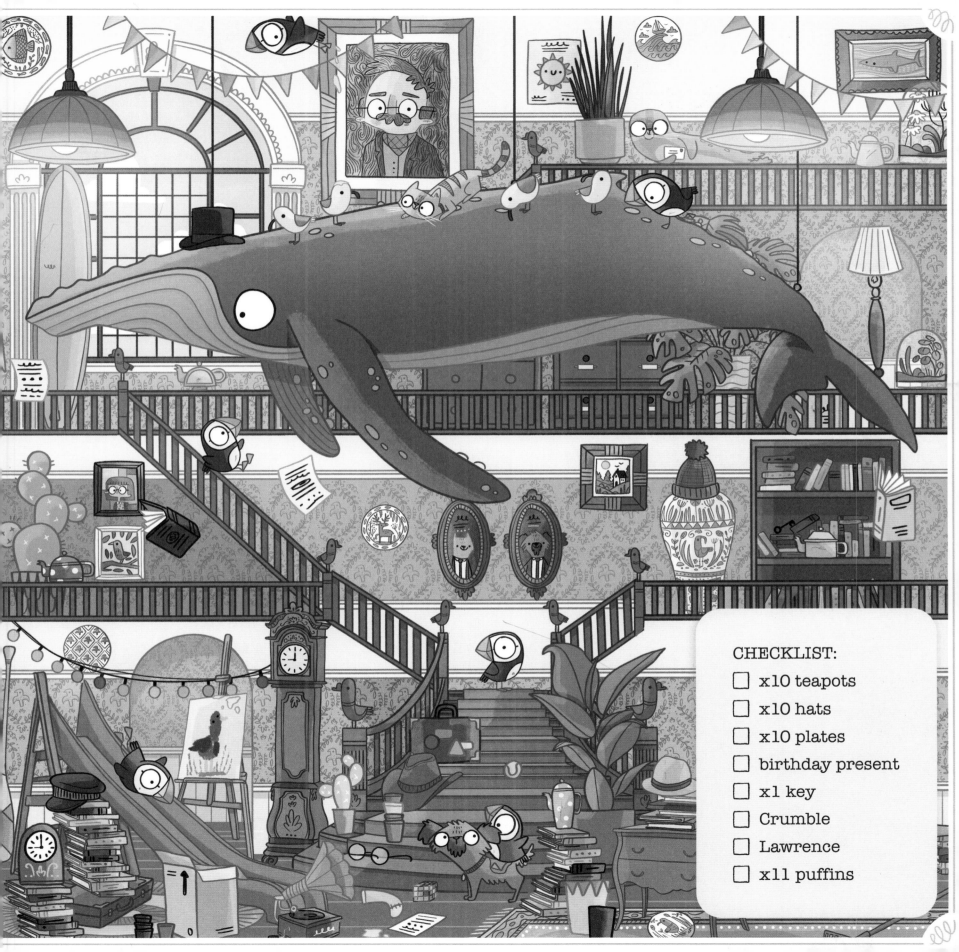

CHECKLIST:

- [ ] x10 teapots
- [ ] x10 hats
- [ ] x10 plates
- [ ] birthday present
- [ ] x1 key
- [ ] Crumble
- [ ] Lawrence
- [ ] x11 puffins

FAO: Penelope
Strudel

CUSTARD INDUSTRIES

Custard Manor
Trifle Hill
Puddington

Dearest Penelope,

If you're reading this then it means you found Tina the Seal and the
letter containing your next clue. Marvellous! Tina can be a slippery
character sometimes so well done for not letting her slip and slide
away from you!

The next clue should be easy for a clever sausage like you. Once
you solve the puzzle it will reveal which room you need to visit
next to bring you one step closer to your birthday surprise.

Lots of love,

Derek

CLUE TWO:

Tina the Seal knows the way to the next room where you'll find the letter and clue you need. Only one line will bring you to the right door. Use your finger to trace the line to the correct answer – can you find it without getting lost?

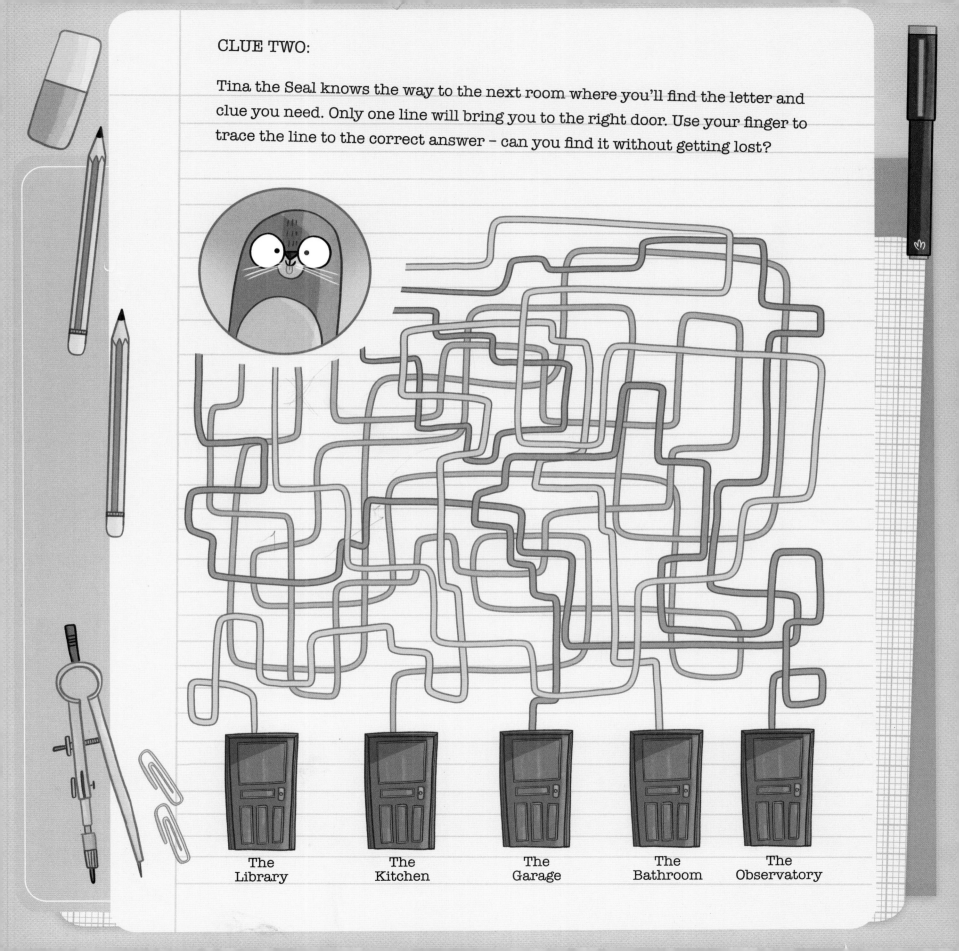

| The Library | The Kitchen | The Garage | The Bathroom | The Observatory |

TOP SECRET

The Kitchen

Oh crikey! What a mess those puffins have made of my lovely kitchen! Those bothersome birds are always trying to steal my breakfast cereal.

Roy the Sloth is keeping the next clue safe for you and is hiding somewhere in the kitchen from all this chaos. He's probably found a tasty snack to munch on while you track him down.

Watch out for flying bananas and whizzing oranges and don't forget to find everything on the checklist!

Derek

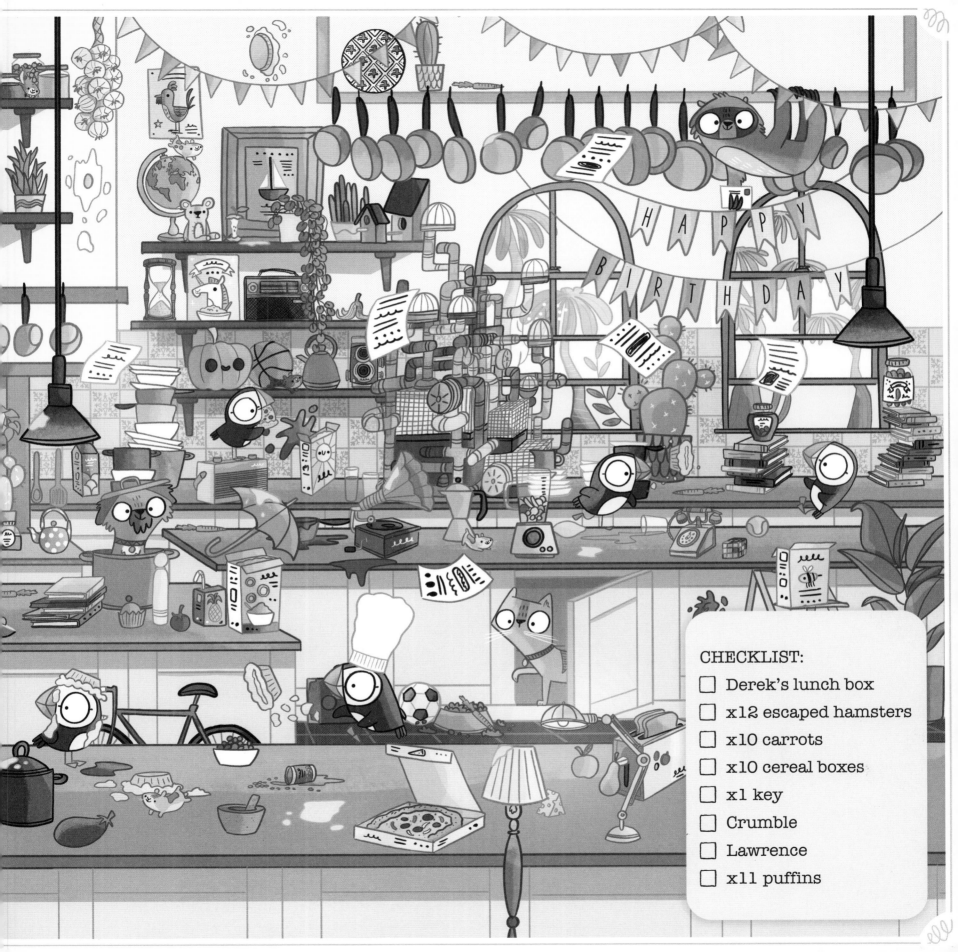

CHECKLIST:
- [ ] Derek's lunch box
- [ ] x12 escaped hamsters
- [ ] x10 carrots
- [ ] x10 cereal boxes
- [ ] x1 key
- [ ] Crumble
- [ ] Lawrence
- [ ] x11 puffins

CUSTARD
INDUSTRIES

Custard Manor
Trifle Hill
Puddington

Dearest Penelope,

What ho! Well done for making it out of the kitchen without getting any food on you – puffins and escaped hamsters combined create quite the mess!

I'm glad to see you found the next clue. I hope Roy the Sloth wasn't too much of a handful – he can be a real party animal sometimes! Well, in between snoozes of course.

You'll have to look very carefully if you're going to solve the next clue. If anyone can do it, you can!

Lots of love,

Derek

CLUE THREE:

Look carefully at the cereal boxes below (full of my most favourite cereal I might add!). Can you spot which one is the odd one out? This mismatched box holds the answer to the next room you need to visit to bring you one step closer to your birthday surprise.

Bedroom

Garage

Museum

Library

Bathroom

Orangery

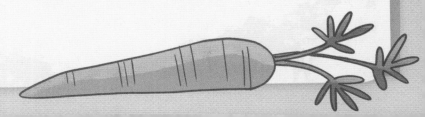

The Library

You solved the clue! Jolly good show! Welcome to my beautiful library... well, it's usually much tidier than this! Make sure you watch out for falling books – those puffins might look adorable but they are up to no good!

Barry the Anteater is hidden somewhere amongst all my many, many books. He's got the next clue for you – can you find him? And don't forget about that checklist!

Derek

P.S. If you get a chance, please can you make sure Crumble isn't chewing everything? He loves the Classics...

CHECKLIST:

- [ ] Derek's teddy bear
- [ ] x10 trophies
- [ ] x12 cups of tea
- [ ] x10 clocks
- [ ] x1 key
- [ ] birthday cake
- [ ] Crumble
- [ ] Lawrence
- [ ] x11 puffins

TOP SECRET

FAO: Penelope
Strudel

CUSTARD INDUSTRIES

Custard Manor
Trifle Hill
Puddington

Dearest Penelope,

Hurrah! You found Barry the Anteater and the next clue.
Well done! Not an easy thing to do with all those books
whizzing around. Those puffins really have made quite the
mess of my poor library. I think Crumble and Lawrence are
going to have to help me re-alphabetise all my beautiful books.

But we're not here to talk about my mint condition volume
of *A to Z of Custard Creams*! It's time to crack the next clue
so you can carry on to the next room and move that much
closer to your birthday surprise!

Lots of love,

Derek

CUSTARD LIBRARY

AUTHOR:	VICTORIA SPONGE
TITLE:	101 THINGS TO DO WITH CUSTARD

DUE DATE:	BORROWER'S NAME
02 · 04	BARRY ANTEATER
06 · 06	DALE T-REX
01 · 09	THE PUFFIN KING

LIBRARY CARD

NAME: DEREK CUSTARD

ADDRESS: CUSTARD MANOR

MEMBER NO: 0001

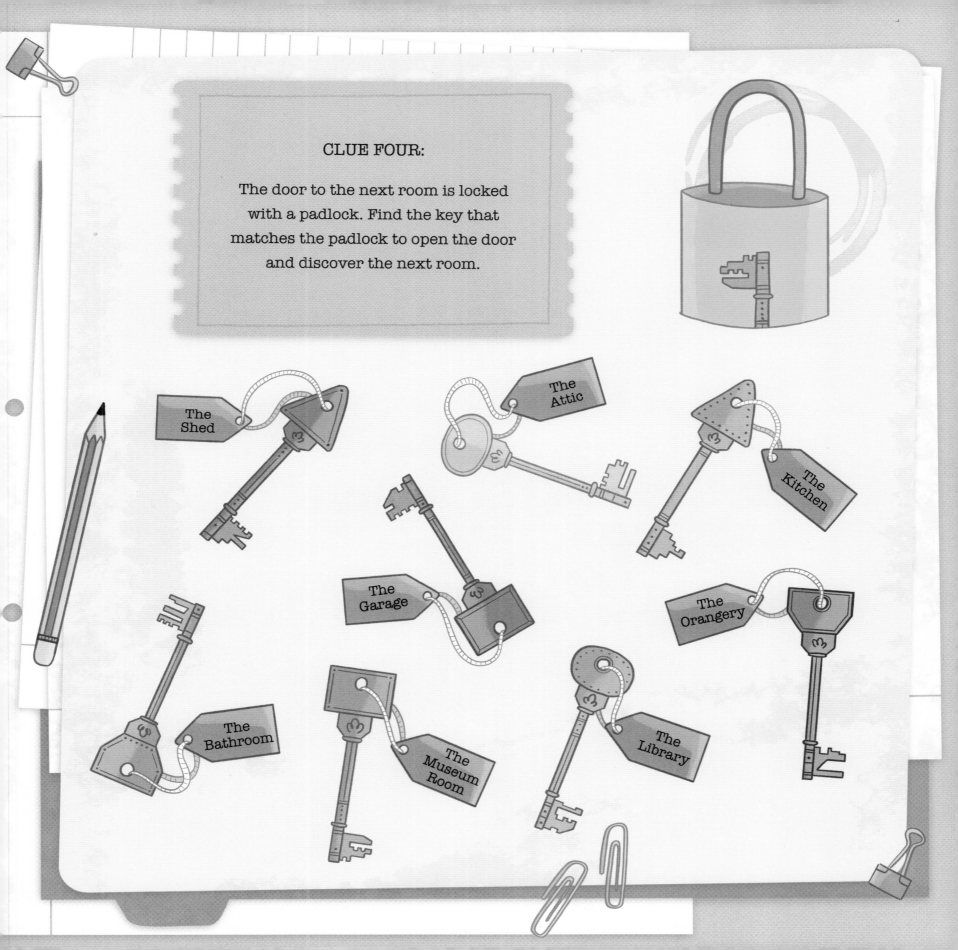

CLUE FOUR:

The door to the next room is locked with a padlock. Find the key that matches the padlock to open the door and discover the next room.

The Shed

The Attic

The Kitchen

The Garage

The Orangery

The Bathroom

The Museum Room

The Library

The Museum Room

By George you've got a knack for cracking these codes. Welcome to my ancient Museum Room! You'll need to watch your step in here. I don't want you to fall into the arms (or worse, mouth) of one of my dinosaur fossils. Keep a special eye out for Dale the T-Rex. He can be awfully grumpy sometimes.

Gwen the Tortoise is hiding somewhere with the next clue. Find her, stop those puffins from breaking any precious artefacts and don't forget to tick off everything on your checklist.

Derek

CHECKLIST:
- [ ] Derek's lost bow tie
- [ ] x12 toy dinosaurs
- [ ] x10 Viking helmets
- [ ] x8 ancient vases
- [ ] birthday hat
- [ ] x1 key
- [ ] Crumble
- [ ] Lawrence
- [ ] x11 puffins

FAO: Penelope Strudel

CUSTARD INDUSTRIES

Custard Manor
Trifle Hill
Puddington

Dearest Penelope,

If you're reading this then it means that Dale the T-Rex hasn't eaten you... YET! Only joking – he's actually a vegetarian so nothing to worry about (although he is quite partial to one of my world-famous custard creams).

Well done for tracking down Gwen the Tortoise. She may not look fast but she can be surprisingly swift when she wants to be. Never underestimate a determined tortoise!

The next clue involves a spot of maths so get your thinking cap on and get ready to add up your answer. It should be no problem for a genius like you!

Lots of love,

Derek

DO NOT DISTURB

There are a few numbers missing in these equations. Find the numbers that should be on the back of each dinosaur. These numbers then match up with one of the combination padlocks at the bottom of the page. Can you work out which room to go to next?

$$? + 3 = 6$$

$$2 + 5 = ?$$

$$3 + ? = 4$$

$$6 + 3 = ?$$

Dining Room · Greenhouse · Bedroom · Storage Cupboard

Derek's Bedroom

Oh Golly. Well this is embarrassing. What a terrible mess my bedroom is. Please avert your eyes from my many pairs of pants – I was in the middle of tidying when you arrived, I swear!

Sirrell the Squirrel is tucked away somewhere in my room. Find him and get the next clue so you can get out of this mess and on to the next room!

Derek

P.S. If you spot scruffy old Crumble sleeping on my bed, could you ask him to move? He can be a very smelly old chap sometimes.

CHECKLIST:

- [ ] Derek's false teeth
- [ ] x12 toy trains
- [ ] x10 boxer shorts
- [ ] x10 tennis balls
- [ ] birthday present
- [ ] x1 key
- [ ] Crumble
- [ ] Lawrence
- [ ] x11 puffins

CUSTARD
INDUSTRIES

Custard Manor
Trifle Hill
Puddington

Dearest Penelope,

I hope this is you reading, and not one of those good-for-nothing
puffins. If so, well done on finding sneaky Sirrell and the sixth
clue amongst all those pants! You're an absolute natural at this.
Keep going!

You shouldn't have much problem with this next clue as you
have already proven your talents for problem solving.

Lots of love,

Derek

CLUE SIX:

The next puzzle involves naming things from around my house and filling in the blank letters in the puzzle below. The letters that go in the yellow squares spell out the name of the next room in your quest. I'm sure you can figure it out! Good luck!

1.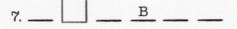

2.

3.

5.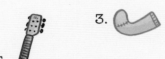

7.

8.

11.

1. B ☐ __ __

2. __ M ☐ __ __ __ __ __ A

3. ☐ __ __ __ K

4. C __ __ ☐

5. __ U __ T __ ☐

6. ☐ __ S __

7. __ ☐ __ B __ __ __

8. T __ __ __ P __ ☐

9. F ☐ __ __ __ __ __ L L

10. __ ☐ __ P H __

11. __ E ☐

4.

6.

9.

10.

The Observatory

Crikey! You're doing a spiffing job at cracking these codes – although I'd expect nothing less from a clever clogs like yourself. Keep up the great work and you'll have beaten those puffins to your birthday surprise in no time!

Welcome to my Observatory. This is one of my favourite rooms but you'll need to keep your eyes peeled – I think I spotted an alien in here once! Try and find Duncan the Deer for your next clue. He's a master of camouflage but I'm sure you'll find him! And as always, stop these feathered foes before they make a complete mess of everything!

Derek

CHECKLIST:
- ☐ Derek's watch
- ☐ x12 toy rockets
- ☐ x5 aliens
- ☐ x10 satellite dishes
- ☐ birthday candles
- ☐ x1 key
- ☐ Crumble
- ☐ Lawrence
- ☐ x11 puffins

FAO: Penelope
Strudel

CUSTARD
INDUSTRIES

Custard Manor
Trifle Hill
Puddington

Dearest Penelope,

Bravo! Good work on navigating your way through my
Observatory. I know how easy it can be to get distracted by
all those big, beautiful telescopes. And I still swear that there
are little mischievous aliens in there... did you spot any?

But I digress – on to the next clue! Well done for spotting
Duncan the Deer. He is a master of disguise so it's not always
an easy thing to do! Now it's time to solve the next clue and
find your way ever closer to your BIG birthday surprise!

I do hope Crumble and Lawrence are helping you with
all these clues and not just snoozing on the job!

Lots of love,

Derek

CLUE SEVEN:

Can you solve this tricky maths problem? The answer will tell you what number door you need to go through to get to the next room and find your next clue.

IF

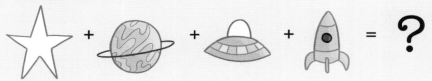

★ + ★ = 20

🪐 + 🪐 + 🪐 = 15

🛸 + 🛸 + 🛸 + 🛸 = 8

🚀 + 🚀 + 🚀 + 🚀 + 🚀 = 15

WHAT IS THE SUM OF

★ + 🪐 + 🛸 + 🚀 = ?

TOP TIP:

If you get stuck then count up the number of lights Duncan has got tangled in his antlers.

Now choose the door with the correct number to continue the Birthday Treasure Hunt!

 30
Study

 20
Bathroom

 25
Treehouse

 50
Games room

The Bathroom

Welcome to my bathroom – I hope you remembered to pack your goggles! I know it's a little different to the usual humdrum toilets you see but who wants to be normal? Not me!

Susan the Shark can look a bit scary but I promise you she is as tame as a mouse! But maybe just stay out of her way to be on the safe side. You'll need to find Beaky Steve the Platypus for your next clue. Don't forget to tick off everything on your checklist – and as always, try and stay well away from those bothersome birds!

Derek

CHECKLIST:

☐ x6 lost socks
☐ x12 rubber ducks
☐ x8 starfish
☐ x6 jellyfish
☐ balloon dog
☐ x1 key
☐ Crumble
☐ Lawrence
☐ x11 puffins

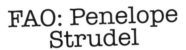

FAO: Penelope Strudel

CUSTARD INDUSTRIES

Custard Manor
Trifle Hill
Puddington

Dearest Penelope,

Hats off to you on finding Beaky Steve the Platypus amongst all those friendly fish. Now you've got the next clue you know what to do!

The next puzzle is a tricky one. Hopefully it will confuse those good-for-nothing puffins! But I know you'll be able to work it out.

Keep going – you're doing brilliantly and getting closer and closer to your wonderful birthday surprise with every step!

Lots of love,

Derek

CLUE EIGHT:

I've created a coded message for you. Use the key below to work out what the message says. Good luck!

KEY

Coded text to original text

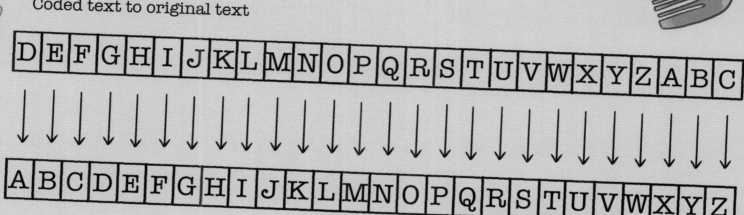

Coded Message

QRZ JR WR WKH

FXVWDUG IDFWRUB

Bonus Message

GRQW OHW WKH SRRLQJ

SXIILQV EHDW BRX WKHUH!

Don't forget to use a sheet of paper to help with this clue!

The Custard Factory

You solved another clue! Well done old sport! Not that I ever doubted you in the slightest.

Welcome to the Custard Factory! This is the greatest room in the entire house. It's in here that I create my world-famous, spectacularly delicious, delightfully scrumptious custard! Of course the recipe is a family secret so make sure those puffins don't find it.

Can you find Percy the Pangolin? He's keeping your next clue safe and sound down here. Oh and for heaven's sake, don't let those puffins poo in my custard!

Derek

CUSTARD
INDUSTRIES

Custard Manor
Trifle Hill
Puddington

Dearest Penelope,

Did you mange to keep those sneaky sea birds and their poo
out of my beautiful custard? My goodness I hope so, otherwise
it will all be ruined!

Well done on finding Percy the Pangolin and the next clue.
He has an extra special love for my custard so I often find
him squirrelled away in my factory with sticky paws!

Now it's on to solving the next clue and moving another step
closer to your wonderful birthday surprise. You're getting
very, very close now – just a few more puzzles to go!

Lots of love,

Derek

CUSTARD
INDUSTRIES

Finest
Award winning
CUSTARD

CLUE NINE:

To solve the next clue, you must use the chart below to work out what the coded message says. Each picture in the message corresponds to a letter. Match them up to find out where the next clue is. Don't forget to use a pen and paper to work it out. Good luck!

A B C D E F
G H I J K L
M N O P Q R
S T U V W X
Y Z

Coded message

THE NEXT CLUE

IS IN THE

ORANGERY

The Orangery

You cracked the code! Well done, but those bothersome birds are here already making a mess. Look at all that poo!

Welcome to the Orangery – it can get a bit hot in here! I used to love coming in here for a dip in the pool but look at what the ducks have done to it. Why do I have such bad luck with birds?

Graham the Giraffe is in here somewhere with your next clue. Find him and you'll be oh so close to your birthday surprise!

Derek

CHECKLIST:
- [ ] runaway hamster
- [ ] x8 wellington boots
- [ ] x10 birdhouses
- [ ] x10 watering cans
- [ ] x4 cupcakes
- [ ] x1 key
- [ ] Crumble
- [ ] Lawrence
- [ ] x11 puffins

CUSTARD INDUSTRIES

Custard Manor
Trifle Hill
Puddington

Dearest Penelope,

So far, so good – you're nearly there now! You've only got a few more clues to solve before you finally find your big birthday surprise!

Well done for finding Graham the Giraffe – I hope you didn't have to strain too much to reach up his tall neck for your clue!

But there's no time to lose – get cracking on the next clue and you'll be on to the next room in no time! I know you can do it!

Lots of love,

Derek

Can you crack the coded message below? Use the code breaker to match the numbers written on the birdhouses to the numbers in the grid. When you match them correctly it will reveal the name of the next room!

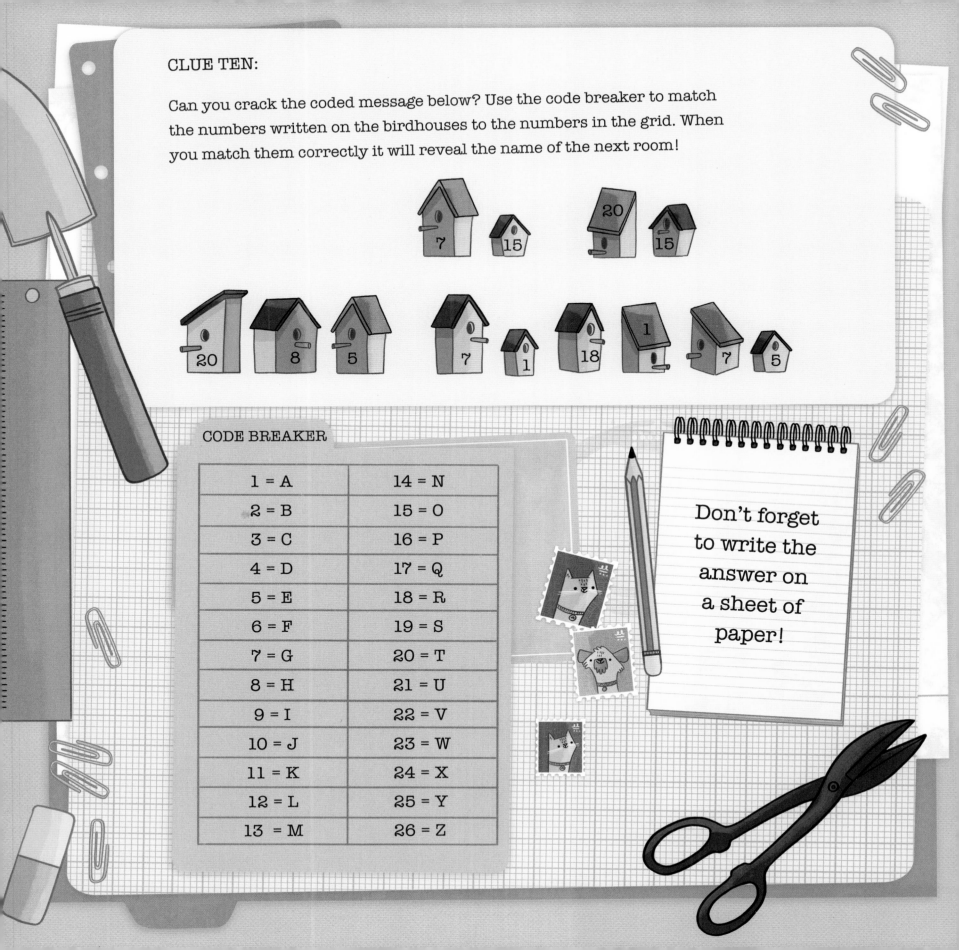

CODE BREAKER

1 = A	14 = N
2 = B	15 = O
3 = C	16 = P
4 = D	17 = Q
5 = E	18 = R
6 = F	19 = S
7 = G	20 = T
8 = H	21 = U
9 = I	22 = V
10 = J	23 = W
11 = K	24 = X
12 = L	25 = Y
13 = M	26 = Z

Don't forget to write the answer on a sheet of paper!

TOP SECRET

The Garage

Wow, I'm impressed! You're almost there now! This is my wonderful Garage, where I keep all of my beloved cars. I hope those beastly birds aren't pooing all over the place – I've just had my cars cleaned!

Doris the Tapir has your final clue. Find her, crack the puzzle and your birthday surprise will be revealed! As always be careful of those silly puffins and keep your eyes peeled for my missing spanners!

Derek

CHECKLIST:
- [ ] Crumble's bone
- [ ] x12 toy cars
- [ ] x11 traffic cones
- [ ] x10 spanners
- [ ] birthday card
- [ ] x1 key
- [ ] Crumble
- [ ] Lawrence
- [ ] x11 puffins

CUSTARD
INDUSTRIES

Custard Manor
Trifle Hill
Puddington

Dear Penelope,

Congratulations on making it so far and thanks for finding
my spanners! I hope you have managed to outwit all of the
silly sea birds!

I have one final puzzle for you. You will need to make your
way through the maze outside. Your birthday surprise is
waiting for you on the other side. Doris loves the maze,
so make sure you bring her too!

Good luck!

See you very soon!

Derek

CLUE ELEVEN:

Using your finger, trace a path through the maze below. Begin at the 'START' sign and try not to take too many wrong turns! Your birthday surprise is waiting for you on the other side! Good luck!

START

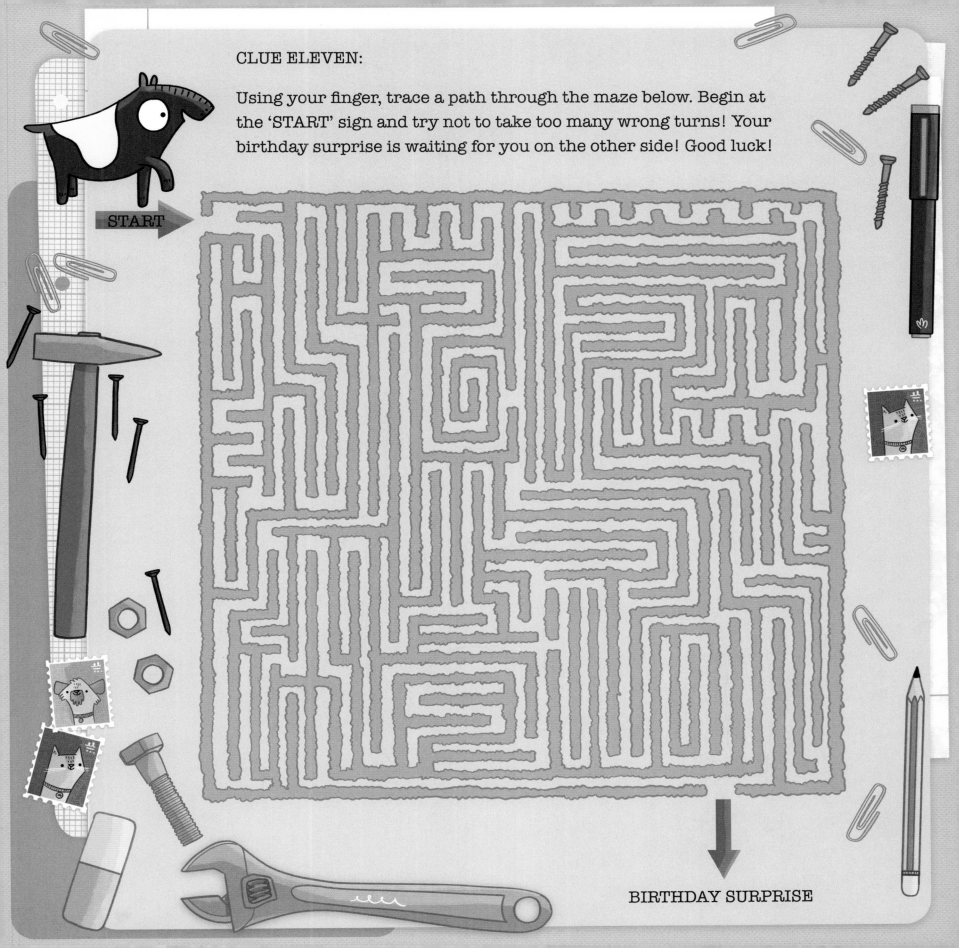

BIRTHDAY SURPRISE

SURPRISE!!!

Hurrah! You solved all the clues and finally found us! What a clever sausage you are!

And look! Those pesky, good-for-nothing puffins are not as bad as we thought. They were only trying to beat you here so that they could join the party!

Now, who wants a slice of cake?

ANSWERS

Did you find some of those search and finds a little tricky? Have no fear, the answers are here! Everything you need has been circled and highlighted below. Keep your wits about you though – those pesky puffins may have been in on your birthday surprise, but they will be after your cake next!

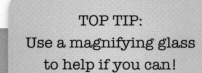
TOP TIP:
Use a magnifying glass
to help if you can!

The Entrance Hall

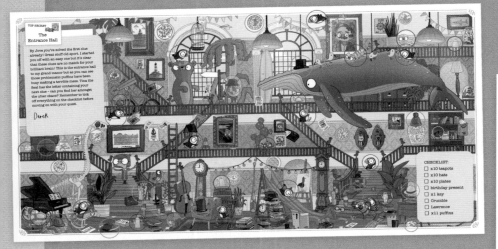

The Kitchen

The Library

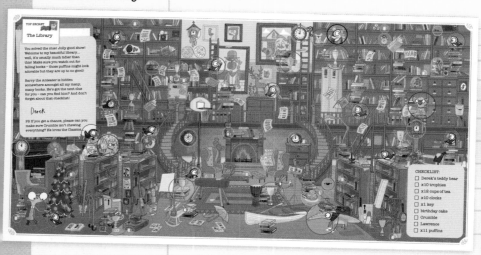

The Museum Room

Derek's Bedroom

Derek's Bedroom

Oh Golly. Well this is embarrassing. What a terrible mess my bedroom is. Please avert your eyes from my many pairs of pants - I was in the middle of tidying when you arrived, I swear!

Sirrell the Squirrel is tucked away somewhere in my room. Find him and get the next clue so you can get out of this mess and on to the next room!

Derek

PS If you spot scruffy old Crumble sleeping on my bed could you ask him to move? He can be a very smelly old chap sometimes.

CHECKLIST:
- ☐ Derek's false teeth
- ☐ x12 toy trains
- ☐ x10 boxer shorts
- ☐ x10 tennis balls
- ☐ birthday present
- ☐ x1 key
- ☐ Crumble
- ☐ Lawrence
- ☐ x11 puffins

The Observatory

The Observatory

Crikey! You're doing a spiffing job at cracking these codes - although I'd expect nothing less from a clever clogs like yourself. Keep up the great work and you'll have beaten those puffins to your birthday surprise in no time!

Welcome to my Observatory. This is one of my favourite rooms but you'll need to keep your eyes peeled - I think I spotted an alien in here come! Try and find Duncan the Deer for your next clue. He's a master of camouflage but I'm sure you'll find him! And as always, stop these feathered foes before they make a complete mess of everything!

Derek

CHECKLIST:
- ☐ Derek's watch
- ☐ x12 toy rockets
- ☐ x5 aliens
- ☐ x10 satellite dishes
- ☐ birthday candles
- ☐ x1 key
- ☐ Crumble
- ☐ Lawrence
- ☐ x11 puffins

The Bathroom

The Bathroom

Welcome to my bathroom - I hope you remembered to pack your gogglos! I know it's a little different to the usual humdrum toilets you use but who wants to be normal?! Not me!

Susan the Shark can look a bit scary but I promise you she is as tame as a mouse! But maybe just stay out of her way to be on the safe side. You'll need to find Beaky Steve the Platypus for your next clue. And don't forget to tick off everything on your checklist and as always, try and stay well away from those bothersome birds!

Derek

CHECKLIST:
- ☐ x6 lost socks
- ☐ x12 rubber ducks
- ☐ x8 starfish
- ☐ x6 jellyfish
- ☐ balloon dog
- ☐ x1 key
- ☐ Crumble
- ☐ Lawrence
- ☐ x11 puffins

The Custard Factory

The Custard Factory

You solved another clue! Well done old sport! Not that I ever doubted you in the slightest.

Welcome to the Custard Factory! This is the greatest room in the entire house. It's in here that I create my world-famous, spectacularly delicious, delightfully scrumptious custard! Of course the recipe is a family secret so make sure those puffins don't find it.

Can you find Percy the Pangolin? He's keeping your next clue safe and sound down here. Oh and for heaven's sake, don't let those puffins poo in my custard!

Derek

CHECKLIST:
- ☐ Derek's rollerskates
- ☐ x10 posters
- ☐ x10 banana skins
- ☐ x5 trumpets
- ☐ birthday dress
- ☐ x1 key
- ☐ Crumble
- ☐ Lawrence
- ☐ x11 puffins

The Orangery

The Orangery

You cracked the code! Well done but those bothersome birds are here already making a mess. Look at all that poo!

Welcome to the Orangery - it can get a bit hot in here! I used to love coming in here for a dip in the pool but look at what the ducks have done to it. Why do I have such bad luck with birds?

Graham the Giraffe is in here somewhere with your next clue. Find him and you'll be oh so close to your birthday surprise!

Derek

CHECKLIST:
- ☐ runaway hamster
- ☐ x8 wellington boots
- ☐ x10 birdhouses
- ☐ x10 watering cans
- ☐ x4 cupcakes
- ☐ x1 key
- ☐ Crumble
- ☐ Lawrence
- ☐ x11 puffins

The Garage

The Garage

Wow, I'm impressed! You're almost there now! This is my wonderful Garage where I keep all of my beloved cars. I hope those beastly birds aren't pooing all over the place - I've just had my cars cleaned!

Doris the Tapir has your final clue. Find her, crack the puzzle and your birthday surprise will be revealed! As always be careful of those silly puffins and keep your eyes peeled for my missing spanners!

Derek

CHECKLIST:
- ☐ Crumble's bone
- ☐ x12 toy cars
- ☐ x11 traffic cones
- ☐ x10 spanners
- ☐ birthday card
- ☐ x1 key
- ☐ Crumble
- ☐ Lawrence
- ☐ x11 puffins

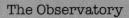

ANSWERS CONTINUED

CLUE ONE:

ENTRANCE HALL

CLUE TWO:

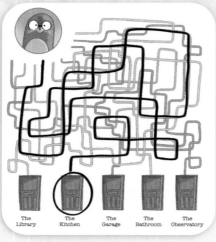

The Library · The Kitchen · The Garage · The Bathroom · The Observatory

CLUE THREE:

Bedroom · Garage · Museum

Library · Bathroom · Orangery

CLUE FOUR:

CLUE FIVE:

3 + 3   6
2 + 5   7
3 + 1   4
6 + 3   9

Dining Room · Greenhouse · Bedroom · Storage Cupboard

CLUE SIX:

b**O** at
um**B** rella
S ock
cak**E**
guita**R**
V ase
r**A** bbit
teap**O** t
f**O** otball
t**R** ophy
ke**Y**

CLUE SEVEN:

★ + 🪐 + 🛸 + 🚀 = 20

30   20   25   50
Study · Bathroom · Greenhouse · Games room

CLUE EIGHT:

DEFGHIJKLMNOPQRSTUVWXYZABC
↓↓↓↓↓↓↓↓↓↓↓↓↓↓↓↓↓↓↓↓↓↓↓↓↓↓
ABCDEFGHIJKLMNOPQRSTUVWXYZ

coded message

NOW GO TO THE
CUSTARD FACTORY

bonus message

DONT LET THE POOING
PUFFINS BEAT YOU THERE

CLUE NINE:

the next clue
is in the
orangery

CLUE TEN:

go to
the garage

CLUE ELEVEN:

Penelope Strudel © 2020 Quarto Publishing plc.
Text and Illustrations © 2020 Brendan Kearney.

First Published in 2020 by Frances Lincoln Children's Books, an imprint of The Quarto Group. The Old Brewery, 6 Blundell Street, London N7 9BH, UK.
T (0)20 7700 6700 F (0)20 7700 8066 www.QuartoKnows.com

The right of Brendan Kearney to be identified as the illustrator of this work has been asserted by him in accordance with the Copyright,
Designs and Patents Act, 1988 (United Kingdom).

A catalogue record for this book is available from the British Library.

ISBN 978-0-7112-5429-9

Set in American Typewriter.

Published by Katie Cotton. Designed by Karissa Santos and Kate Haynes. Production by Dawn Cameron. Edited by Claire Grace and Alex Hithersay.

Manufactured in Guangdong, China EB022021
9 8 7 6 5 4 3 2 1